This book is dedicated to
T. R. Geisel of Springfield, Mass.,
The World's Greatest Authority
on Blackfish, Fiddler Crabs and Deegel Trout

McELLIGOT'S POOL

Written and illustrated by DR. SEUSS

RANDOM HOUSE  NEW YORK

This title was originally cataloged by the Library of Congress as follows:
[Geisel, Theodor Seuss] 1904– McElligot's pool, written and illustrated by Dr. Seuss [pseud.]
New York, Random House [1947] [56] p. illus (part col.) 20 cm.
I. Title. PZ8.3.G276Mac 47-4895 ISBN: 0-394-80083-4 (trade) ; 0-394-90083-9 (lib. bdg.)

Manufactured in the United States of America

67 69 71 70 72 68 66

Young man," laughed the farmer,
"You're sort of a fool!
You'll *never* catch fish
In McElligot's Pool!"

"The pool is too small.
And, you might as well know it,
When people have junk
Here's the place that they throw it.

"You might catch a boot
Or you might catch a can.
You might catch a bottle,
But listen, young man...
If you sat fifty years
With your worms and your wishes,
You'd grow a long beard
Long before you'd catch fishes!"

"Hmmm…" answered Marco,
"It *may* be you're right.
I've been here three hours
Without one single bite.
There *might* be no fish…

"…But, again,
Well, there *might!*"

"'Cause you never can tell
What goes on down below!

"This pool *might* be bigger
Than you or I know!"

This MIGHT be a pool, like I've read of in books,
Connected to one of those underground brooks!

An underground river that starts here and flows
Right under the pasture! And then...well, *who knows?*

It *might* go along, down where no one can see,
Right under State Highway Two-Hundred-and-Three!
Right under the wagons! Right under the toes
Of Mrs. Umbroso who's hanging out clothes!

It *might* keep on flowing...perhaps...who can tell?...
Right under the people in Sneeden's Hotel!
Right under the grass where they're playing croquet!
Then under the mountains and far, far away!

This *might* be a river,
Now mightn't it be,

       Connecting

          McElligot's

             Pool

                With

                   The

                     Sea!

Then maybe some fish might be swimming toward me!

             (If such a thing *could* be,
             They certainly *would* be!)

Some very smart fellow might point out the way
To the place where I'm fishing. And that's why I say
If I wait long enough; if I'm patient and cool,
Who knows *what* I'll catch in McElligot's Pool!

I might catch a thin fish,

I might catch a stout fish.

I might catch a short

or
a
long,
long
drawn-out fish!

Any kind! Any shape! Any color or size!
I *might* catch some fish that would open your eyes!

I won't be surprised if a *Dog Fish* appears!
Complete with a collar and long floppy ears!
Whoofing along! And perhaps he might chase
A whole lot of *Catfish* right straight to this place!

I might catch a fish
With a pinwheel-like tail!

I might catch a fish
Who has fins like a sail!

I might catch some young fish
Some high-jumping friskers.

I might catch an old one
With long flowing whiskers!

I might catch a fish
With a long curly nose.

I might catch a fish
Like a rooster that crows.

I might catch a fish
With a checkerboard belly,

Or even a fish
Made of strawberry jelly!

I might catch a Sea Horse.

(Now mightn't I now...?)

I might catch a fish
Who is partly a cow!

Some fish from the Tropics, all sunburned and hot,
Might decide to swim up!

Well they might...
Might they not?

Racing up north for a chance to get cool,
Full steam ahead for McElligot's Pool!

Some Eskimo Fish
From beyond Hudson Bay
Might decide to swim down;
Might be headed this way!

It's a pretty long trip,
But they *might*
And they *may*.

I might catch an eel...
(Well, I might. It depends.)
...A long twisting eel
With a lot of strange bends
And, oddly enough,
With a head on both ends!

One doesn't catch *this* kind of fish as a rule,
But the chances are fine in McElligot's Pool!

I might catch a fish
With a terrible grouch...

Or an Australian fish
With a kangaroo's pouch!

Who wants to catch small ones like mackerel or trout!
SAY! I'll catch a Saw Fish with such a long snout
That he needs an assistant to help him about!

If I wait long enough, if I'm patient and cool,
Who knows *what* I'll catch in McElligot's Pool!

Some rough-neck old Lobster,
All gristle and muscle,
Might grab at my bait,
Then would I have a tussle!

To land one so tough might take two or three hours,
But the *next* might be easy...

...The kind that likes flowers.

I *might* catch some sort of a fast-moving bloke
Who zips through the waves with an over-arm stroke!

(I *might* and I *may* and that's really no joke!)

A fish even faster!
A fish, if you please,
Who slides down the sides
Of strange islands on skis!

He *might* ski on over and pay me a visit.
That's not impossible...really, now is it?

Some Circus Fish!
Fish from an acrobat school,
Might stage a big show in McElligot's Pool!

Or I might catch a fish
From a stranger place yet!
From the world's highest river
In far-off Tibet,
Where the falls are so steep
That it's dangerous to ride 'em,
So the fish put up chutes
And they float down beside 'em.

From the world's deepest ocean,

From way down below,

From down in the mud where the deep-divers go,

From down in the mire and the muck and the murk,

I might catch some fish who are all going, "GLURK!"

WHALES!

I'll catch whales!

Yes, a whole herd of whales!

All spouting their spouts

And all thrashing their tails!

I'll catch fifty whales,

Then I'll stop for the day

'Cause there's *nothing* that's bigger

Than whales, so they say.

Still, of course,
It *might* be...

…that there IS something bigger!
Some sort of a kind of
A THING-A-MA-JIGGER!!

A fish that's so big, if you know what I mean,
That he makes a whale look like a tiny sardine!

Oh, the sea is so full of a number of fish,
If a fellow is patient, he *might* get his wish!

And that's why I think
That I'm not such a fool
When I sit here and fish
In McElligot's Pool!

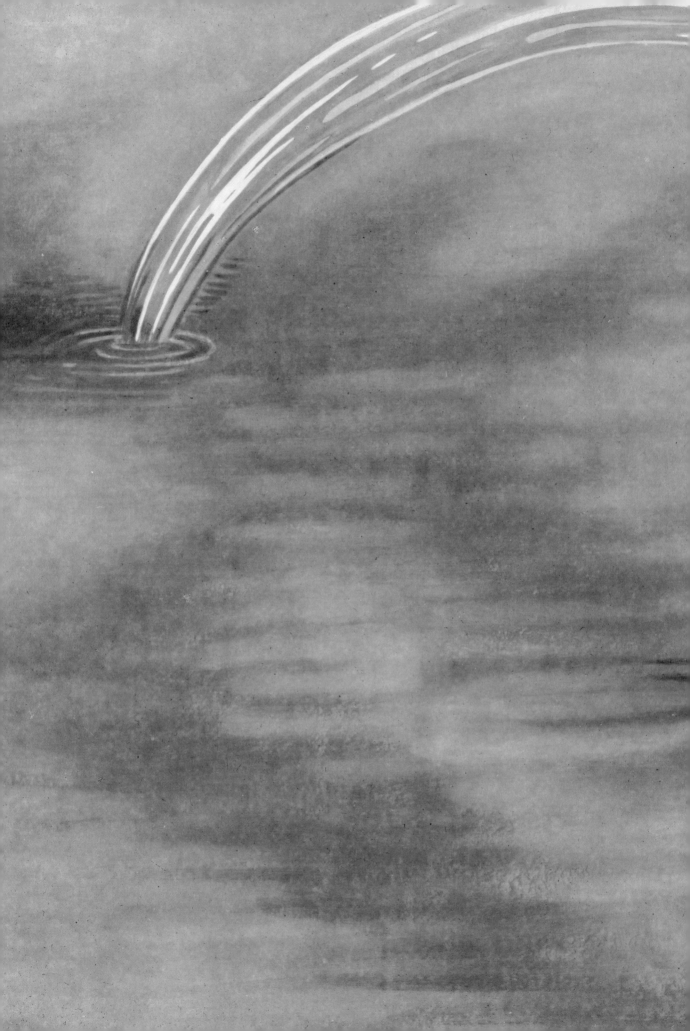